ZOO BOY

SOPHIE THOMPSON

is an Olivier Award-winning actress. Her films include *Harry Potter and the Deathly Hallows*, *Emma*, *Persuasion* and *Four Weddings and a Funeral*. On stage Sophie has appeared in many plays and musicals at the National Theatre, RSC and in the West End. Her television roles have included *The Detectorists*, *Jericho* and *EastEnders*. Sophie won Celebrity MasterChef in 2014 and wrote the cookbook *My Family Kitchen: Favourite recipes from four generations*. She has two teenage sons and lives in North London. *Zoo Boy* is her debut story for children.

ZOO BOY

SOPHIE THOMPSON

Illustrated by Rebecca Ashdown

ff

FABER & FABER

First published in 2016
by Faber & Faber Limited
Bloomsbury House, 74–77 Great Russell Street
London WC1B 3DA

Typeset by Faber & Faber Limited
Printed and bound in the UK by CPI Group UK (Ltd)
Croydon CR0 4YY

A CIP record for this book is available
from the British Library

ISBN 978–0–571–32224–4

FSC
www.fsc.org
MIX
Paper from
responsible sources
FSC® C101712

1 3 5 7 9 10 8 6 4 2

For Ernie and Walter

One

Hello, dear reader.

Are you sitting, lying down, standing on your head, eating a jam sandwich comfortably?

Then I'll begin . . .

I want to introduce you to a boy called Vince, whose birthday

1

it is today.

Here's some information about him, written by the birthday boy himself, in the new diary given to him by his gran.

Dear diary,

Hello, I am your new friend Vince.

I am now ~~offishally~~ officially eight. Yippety yip. (Gran says it's a magic number.)

Your pages smell nice and I've decided to write in an orange pen today as it's my favourite colour.

I had orange juice for breakfast, freshly sqᵘeezed by Gran as a birthday treat, AND she gave me a whole tin of orange wine gums.

3

It gave Gran a good excuse to eat all the other colours herself. Ha ha. When you are at least a hundred and eight years old you are allowed to do that. Can't wait!

Mum is still off at the circus with that lion keeper man with the silly bobbly ~~mussels~~ muscles, I'm afraid. I was rather hoping that because it's my birthday a miracle might have

happened, and Lion Keeper
Man would have been
eaten by one of
his lions, and she'd
have come home,
but no such luck.
Dad's still very
weepy about the whole
thing. He put on a brave face
this morning, which actually ~~acktully~~ made
me feel even sadder, but it's
perking me up talking to you, dear
diary . . .

Derek. I'll call you Derek.

Anyway, Derek, the only present Dad gave me was . . . wait for it . . . a GOLDFISH!

A goldfish, I ask you. (I suppose it fits in with the orange theme.) I should probably tell you now that I dislike animals intensely but Dad is STILL trying to convert me. It's tragic. I've already lost ~~too~~ two hamsters. Well, when I say lost, they escaped. I think they could sense my lack of commitment. The

6

Great Marzini was clearly never meant to be a pet — he got out of the cage even when it had a padlock on it — and as for Polo, I suspect she ran off to warmer climes as she was forever getting stuck behind the radiator. Anyway, at least I don't have to stroke a silly goldfish. It just swims round and round its bowl like a nutcase. I have 'Supreme Flaked Food' to feed it, which smells very fishy. That doesn't seem right. I certainly wouldn't want to eat any food that smelt like ME.

Just because Dad's WHOLE LIFE is animals — he's a zoo keeper (I know, YUCK! the variety of poo alone is distressing) — he is desperate for me to change a habit of a lifetime . . . well, eight years, to be precise ~~presice~~. Poor, deluded Dad. I suppose, if you want to know, I'm jealous of those grotty,

8

pongy animals and all the attention Dad gives them. Since Mum left he works the whole time! THERE. I've said it. Talking to you is fun, Derek. I can say what I think and not worry about hurting people's feelings.

ANYWAY. As I said, Dad gave me a goldfish. NO balloons, NO cake, just a goldfish. He has officially lost the plot. And Gran has knitted me a massive orange birthday jumper.

I know. Embarrassing. Perhaps I could unravel it accidentally on purpose.

Oh, and I did get a whole tenner in the post from bad Uncle Stanley . . .

'Vince! Vince! Let's go!'

Sorry Derek, must dash. Apparently, now I'm eight it's time I started helping Dad at work. What's that about! Ghastly idea. He says it's a `family tradition`, handed on from father to —

'VINCE!'

Two

Dad was standing
by the back door
looking anxious.

'Come on, son.
What a special day.
I remember when I
first helped my dad,

Grandpa Jacko, at the zoo. I'd just turned eight, too!'

Gran suddenly appeared.

'Oh, my blazing birthday bog nut! Don't forget your birthday jumper. It's important to have high visibility in the workplace.'

She held out the orange jumper with glee. 'Grandpa would be so proud of you!'

'So would your mum,' said Dad, and

started to look a
bit weepy again.

Vince pulled
on the jumper.

Not only was
he having to help
at the zoo but he
looked . . . like
THIS!

Oh dear.

Dad let them through the security
gate at the bottom of the garden with

the magic secret song. Sorry, dear reader, let me explain . . . Dad had to sing the magic secret song, known only to zoo keepers, into a cunningly concealed microphone to unlock the door. (I wish I could divulge further information but currently I've been prevented from sharing this with you by the Powers That Be. I'm working on it, and will keep you in the loop.)

Ten minutes later, Vince was standing in the middle of the

penguin enclosure holding a fat, yellow hose and feeling really horribly orange and itchy. He'd managed to roll his sleeves up but that meant he could barely move his arms.

'Is it coming on?' his dad shouted from over the wall.

'NO!' Vince yelled back crossly.

Then the big, smelly hose started to gurgle ominously. It tightened in Vince's hand and leapt out of his grasp, swivelling about like a demented banana.

'Ahhh!' Vince shrieked as water sprayed all over him.

He was dancing about trying to grab the hose when Dad appeared and shoved it in the pond.

'Got it. Sorry, Vince! Oo-er, you're soaking – better go home and change, buddy. Let me just turn the water off.'

THAT was a result, Vince thought. They'd only been here ten minutes – maybe Dad would forget about 'family traditions' and reveal he'd secretly made a huge vat of birthday-flavoured jelly or something.

He jumped about in the puddles with quiet, hopeful glee.

'Nasty jumper!' chirruped a

bright, plummy voice.

Vince started. Where had that rude remark come from? There was no one there. The zoo was closed because it was Thursday. (It was always closed on a Thursday as the owner belonged to a religious group who weren't allowed to do anything on Thursdays except eat biscuits.)

'Asquith's the name,' the bright voice continued.

Vince swung round to find himself facing a penguin with shiny, raisiny eyes. The penguin was blinking cheekily at him and sporting a rather unexpected pinstriped waistcoat.

'You understand me, don't you, Vince?'

Vince was rooted to the rock. 'Yes,' he heard himself whisper.

'Listen, young fellow, I'll cut to the chase. Need you to get hold of some of these "fish fingers" for me. I'm desperate to

try them. All I ever get here is fish without their fingers and I've heard the fingers are the best bit.'

'Yes, I . . . Shouldn't be a problem,' Vince replied.

Hang on a chicken-lickin' moment . . .

VINCE WAS TALKING TO A PENGUIN.

CONVERSING WITH A PENGUIN.

HE WAS CLEARLY FLUENT IN PENGUIN!

CALL THE AUTHORITIES: THE BOY WAS SUPERHUMAN!

With that, Dad appeared. 'Right! Home-and-dry time, buddy.' Vince watched Asquith jump into the pond and swim gracefully away.

Vince felt a zillion words pressing against his lips and they were all in capital letters – RED ones.

WHY?

WHAT?

AM I DREAMING? . . . were just five of them.

All those words in his head and all of them too big and too red to fit through his mouth. Even if he could speak and explain what had happened, Dad would surely think he was completely unhinged and probably do more crying.

Vince resolved to try to talk to Gran as she WAS completely unhinged and he felt certain SHE would understand about a talking penguin called Asquith.

Three

Dad let them back through the security gate with the magic secret song. (I have been assured it's only a matter of time until it can be revealed, so we must be PATIENT. I'm told it's a virtue.)

Gran was practising her

pirouettes in the kitchen, having changed into an aquamarine cocktail dress with lemon-yellow trim and lots more jewellery.

'Oooh, hello loves, did you have fun?' she asked, clocking Vince. 'Are you all right, my crunchy little conker? You look like a drowned rat that's left its tail on the train without a ticket.'

Vince was trying to remain calm.

'There was a hose situation,' Dad said, sounding rather crestfallen.

'Oooh, you poor rapscallion,' said Gran kindly. 'Get yourself dry before you get a birthday chill. I'll be up in the shake of a shorn sheep's tail to check if you're all right.'

Vince leapt up the stairs two by two, peeled off his wet clothes (it was like peeling a gigantic orange) and put on his panda onesie.

He grabbed Derek the diary, sat on the edge of his bed and frantically began to write:

Derek! Derek! I think I can understand Animal!

ME of all animal-disliking people! The irony!

> A penguin called Asquith was rude about my birthday jumper!
>
> He talked to me and I talked back!
>
> He said he wants fish fingers!

There was a knock at the door. Vince could tell it was Gran by the sound of her earrings clattering.

She came in looking like a bottle of lemonade that had been shaken and was trying not to burst its bubbles out. She settled herself beside Vince without breaking her stare. Her eyes were more sparkly than her jewellery. Her breath smelt of sponge cake.

'You can do it, can't you, Babes? Grandpa Jacko was SURE you would be able to. You've got the gift, haven't you? You can talk to the animals at last.'

He KNEW she'd understand. Dear, mad Gran. But what did she mean about Grandpa Jacko?

Vince had just missed meeting his Grandpa Jacko. He had been born at almost exactly the same moment that Grandpa had died. Curious. Gran always said that some of Grandpa's spirit had hitched a ride with Vince.

'It was HIS gift, Vince,' Gran continued, as though she had heard Vince's thoughts. 'He knew it would be yours and not your dad's. The gift skips a generation, you see, to have a rest. It's hard work being a gift.'

Words tumbled out of Vince like marbles on wheels:

'Oh Gran! A penguin called Asquith asked me for fish fingers –

'He knew my name, Gran –

'He had shiny eyes like beads –

'And he spoke as posh as you like –

'I've never been keen on animals, let alone talked to them –

'I feel like I must have gone loony!'

(Vince left out the bit about Asquith being rude about the jumper, which I think was wise, don't you?)

'You're not loony, my beautiful little monkey wrench. You are the next in line and I couldn't be prouder! What LARKS! It was the thing that made Grandpa his happiest, Vince. Working for the animals. A great responsibility, and such a worthy one. Sometimes I wished so hard I could join him, but I found my delight in the pubs and clubs, dancing and singing, communicating in my own way.' Gran laughed and her earrings tinkled.

'But Gran!' Vince said plaintively. 'I'm only just eight and I'm not a zoo keeper. I don't know the secret song or anything.'

Gran suddenly looked uncharacteristically serious and left the room. When she returned she was holding a yellowy scroll of paper tied with a scrappy piece of red, striped velvet ribbon.

She solemnly handed it to Vince. 'A very happy birthday from Grandpa Jacko.'

Vince carefully unfurled the greasy paper . . .

A very happy
8th birthday!
From Grandpa
Jacko xxx

And there, dear reader, was the Zoo Keepers' Song, written out in brown swirling ink.

'Crikey,' said Vince, sensing that this moment made his birthday rise to mountain-like proportions.

'Crikey,' he repeated as he read the song through.

I have to humbly apologise yet again, dear reader, as I'm still under solemn oath NOT to divulge to you the secret Zoo Keepers' Song. I remain in deep negotiations with the relevant authorities, and when I finally get permission to reveal the contents of that mysterious scroll, please rest assured you will be the first to know what lies within.

'Well, what are you waiting for, my precious polished pumpkin seed? I think Grandpa Jacko would say,

"It's fish finger frying time!'" said Gran, clapping her old hands together like a gleeful seal.

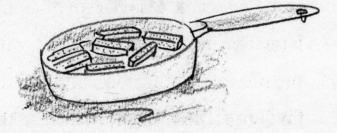

Four

'Where's Dad, Gran?' Vince asked as he watched Gran sizzling the fish fingers in a pan. 'This might just be the perfect news he needs to cheer him up!'

'Oh, he's gone to . . . get some more candy floss. He hoped you wouldn't mind, Vince.'

'I see,' said Vince quietly, knowing exactly what 'candy floss' meant. It was Dad's excuse to spy on Mum

at the circus. And Vince did mind a bit, actually. He had thought on this birthday Dad might have wanted to stay at home with him. That said, it did mean Vince could get on with the pressing business at hand. He'd tell him everything later. He'd make his day!

'Off you go, cherry pip,' said Gran, handing Vince a little warm parcel of fish fingers. 'Grandpa would be giddy with joy to know this historic occasion had arrived. Good luck.'

Vince got to the gate, fished the scroll from his pocket and rather self-consciously sang the Zoo Keepers' Song quietly into the microphone.

The gate kerplinged open.

Vince felt like the king of the castle.

But before he had time to gloat and imagine all the ermine on his cloak and how big his crown should be, an enormous badger who smelt of old socks appeared from the scrubby shrubbery.

'Well, you'll cause a commotion,' the badger said.

'Pardon?' replied Vince.

'ALL the zoo animals will want stuff now. You wait and see. I hope you know what you've let yourself in for. I'm Horace. I'm wild. I just choose to live here.'

A penguin called Asquith. A badger called Horace.

Vince was gawping open-mouthed at

Horace's badgery aroma and gravelly voice when he remembered his manners – 'Oh, how do you do? I'm Vince,' said Vince.

'Yes, mind my worms, you've opened a can of words. These zoo animals ran that Jacko ragged,' said Horace haughtily.

'Jacko! He was my grandpa!'

'Oh good grief, of course!' Horace exclaimed. 'I see the family resemblance now. You're the next in line.'

Vince walked with Horace to the penguin pond, where Asquith was reclining on some pretend rocks, filing his nails in the afternoon sun.

'Asquith!' Vince called out. 'I've brought your fish fingers!'

Asquith jumped up and waddled over, greedily eyeing the package Vince held. And I'm sorry to have to tell you, dear reader, that when he reached Vince, Asquith snatched the fish fingers from him – yes, snatched!

– and waddled away, shovelling the fingers in like a pig. (Don't tell any pigs you know I said that.) And not ONE word of thanks!

Vince shouted lamely after him, 'I really hope you like them.'

Vince looked at Horace.

Horace snorted, 'Mr Manners is clearly on holiday.'

Horace and Vince bade each other farewell at the gate.

'So glad to be acquainted,' said

Horace. 'I must ask – is there a reason you're dressed like a panda?'

(I'd forgotten Vince still had his onesie on, had you?)

'Trying to blend in . . .' replied Vince, fibbing because, in all honesty, he had forgotten he was still wearing it.

Just then, an extremely snooty-looking flamingo emerged from behind a bush, as if she were making an entrance on to a grand stage through a leafy curtain.

'I've heard tell you're the boy who can get us what we want, so listen up, Vincey, young fellah-me-lad . . .' she said, sounding very hoity-toity indeed. 'I want Battenberg cake. Only the pink bits, and I want it NOW. Candy floss, Battenberg, radishes, PINK

FOOD in general, and make it snappy. I'm paling with each day that goes by, and if a flamingo's not pink, she can't hold her head high! Fenella's the name, being pink is my game.'

And with that she trotted off like a swan in overly high heels, wiggling her feathery bottom.

'Crikey!' Vince was quite taken aback. 'She's scarily confident.'

'You should have met her mother,' Horace muttered darkly. 'Monstrous creature. Wore a tiara. But she's just the start. Mark my words, Vince, there'll be many more demands.'

Gran was waiting on tenterhooks by the door and was surprised to see a rather perplexed-looking panda approaching.

'What's wrong, my little desiccated coconut? Didn't the penguin like the fish fingers?' she asked.

'Gran, I don't know, he snatched

them away, and a badger called Horace says I'll cause a commotion, and Fenella, this curious pink bird with a big black beak and very worrying legs, wants LOTS of pink things! I've got to do the right thing, Gran. I can't let Grandpa down.'

Five

Okey dokey, Vince thought, chewing on a cold sausage from the fridge to give himself strength. Radishes for Fenella. No probs. We've got loads in the veg patch. No one ever eats them.

He dug some up.

Pheweee. Digging was tiring.

Okay, um . . . Candy floss. No probs. There were HEAPS of that in the larder, thanks to Dad's visits to the circus. He bought a bag every time, and was probably buying another one right now!

Vince opened the larder door and sure enough twelve bags tumbled out.

Fenella wanted Battenberg, too. No probs. That was Gran's favourite. There was half a one in the cake tin. Vince cut out all the pink bits. 'It looks a mess,' he reflected, 'but it is pink!'

What else? . . . He scoured the cupboard and found:

Pink food colouring.

Pinkish raspberry jelly.

And some cherry jam that was sort of pink . . . Perfect, he thought. Fenella would be pleased.

He ran down to the gate feeling like a panda postman with  his rucksack brimming with pink parcels.

Vince sang the Zoo Keepers' Song with a little more confidence this time and – kerploot! – the door was open.

'Um . . . Fenella!' he shouted rather nervously. 'You really will be pink as you like with all of this, I think!'

Horace sauntered up. 'That rhymed and you look mad,' he mused.

Vince did indeed look quite mad.

He was dressed as a panda. He had soil on his nose from digging the radishes, Battenberg crumbs round his mouth from having to make sure it tasted all right, candy floss in his hair (because it ALWAYS gets there

no matter what, don't you find?),
and a very wild look in his eye.

Fenella clip-clopped up, looking
extremely snooty-boots.

'Here, Fenella,' Vince said
proudly. 'I managed to get everything
you asked for and MORE!'

Fenella picked through his
rucksack, making disgruntled
flamingo noises.

'Well, you've been jolly quick,
I grant you, but that Battenberg
smells stale, those radishes need a

wash, that candy has lost its floss . . .
and what's all this? Food colouring?
How basic! Jelly? How quaint! Jam?
What do I spread that on exactly?'

With that she snorted and turned
on her heels, dragging away all

her booty and shrieking . . .

'HE'S HERE, EVERYONE!'

There was a rustle, and a bustle,

A shoogle and a shunt,

A fizzle and a fussle,

A brimble and a brunt.

SUDDENLY there was a VERY unlikely line-up of animals standing before Vince and Horace, and – you've guessed it – they ALL wanted STUFF!

Six

There was an enormous pig who lolloped up to Vince smelling of old vegetables and boiled rice.

'I'm Carol, get me eggs – free range, mind!' she spluttered.

There was a huge
owl with tiny glasses on,
who waddled up to Vince
looking like a small,
elderly lady (made of
feathers).

'I'm Janet, get me mice, sugar
ones I'm talking about!'
she squawked scornfully.
There was a llama
who danced towards
Vince like a dizzy
donkey, baring a set of

very dodgy-looking gnashers.

'I'm Juan, darlink, geet me sheeeeerbet leeeeemons! Ooh, theeeeese feeeeeezy whizzy leeeeemons and LOTS of theeeeeem, LOTS! I have threeeee stomachs, darleeeeenk!'

'He's from Argentina,' mumbled Horace. 'Very sweet tooth . . . hence the dicky ivories,' he added witheringly.

There was a bald Scottish eagle who flew right up to Vince's head and eyeballed him with piercing eagle eyes. (I have to say, dear reader, Vince did very well not to leap with utter fright!)

'I'm Hamish, get me haggis, I wan' haggis, ge' me two, ge' me three!' he spluttered, whilst another tiny feather quietly pinged out of his balding head.

There was an orangutan who swaggered up to Vince like a boxer

swaggering towards the ring for a fight.

'I'm Terry, get me those coolio chocolate-covered 'nanas, dude. A BIG box, mind. We're talking BULK!'

There was a very frisky goat.

'I'm Dave, get me clover, WILD clover! And some denim shorts!

I'm very partial to denim shorts!
YUM!'

And with that they all

bumbled

gambled

shimmied

and shambled

goopled and

prandled off.

(Have you ever goopled or prandled? I've heard it can be quite fun.)

'Crikey!' Vince exclaimed, feeling

rather overwhelmed. 'I'll have to make a list. I mustn't forget anyone. I bet Grandpa never did . . . I don't want to let anyone down, least of all him!'

And back to the house Vince strode. A panda on a mission.

Horace just stood there for a moment watching the dust settle.

'I feel a tad unwell,' he groaned quietly to himself.

Seven

Vince got Derek the diary and a biro, and settled at the kitchen table to  try and remember what all the animals had asked for.

Here, dear reader, is Vince's first
list:

- pig wants HAGGIS
- owl wants SHORTS
- llama wants SUGAR MICE
- eagle wants EGGS (FREE
  RANGE)
- orangutan wants SHERBET
  LEMONS
- goat wants CLOVER AND
  CHOC BANANA~~S~~

I know . . . He got very muddled and frankly I'm not surprised.

Once he'd had the cup of squash and the yellow bits of Battenberg cake that Gran fetched him, his head began to clear and he tried again:

- pig wants EGGS (FREE RANGE)
- owl wants SUGAR MICE
- llama wants SHERBET LEMONS
- eagle wants HAGGIS

- orangutan wants WILD
  CLOVER AND DENIM
  SHORTS
- goat wants CHOC BANANAS

(I've got the feeling those last two
are still wrong, haven't you?)

This required a trip to the
Everything You Could Possibly
Want For 99p Unless It's Slightly
More Expensive Shop.

'I've got to go to the Everything
You Could Possibly Want For 99p

Unless It's Slightly More Expensive Shop, Gran.'

'All right,' said Gran. 'I'll be poised here like a coiled gazelle with clogs on.'

Vince got his bike and the birthday monies he had been sent by bad Uncle Stanley. (Vince had been going to put it towards some new trainers he wanted but this was MUCH more important. He must sacrifice his needs for the animals. Vince felt sure that's what Grandpa

Jacko would have done.)

Off he rode. It was only down the road (which sounds the same as rode, doesn't it, but spelt differently).

Eight

The Everything You Could Possibly
Want For 99p Unless It's Slightly
More Expensive Shop was run by
a ridiculously cheerful man called
Leviticus   Corkindale   Percival
Calamine   Periwig   Candlewick
Throoob. But everyone just called

him Bob.

'Hello, young fellah me lad,' said Bob, ridiculously cheerfully. 'What can I get you today?'

Bob's shop had a wooden counter running down its entire length and Bob wore roller skates so he could whizz to and fro like a ridiculously cheerful man on roller skates getting you things.

He also had a very small assistant called Ping (who slightly ponged). Ping's job was climbing the ladders to the higher shelves. She was impossibly shy and barely spoke.

'Would you like to see my list, Bob?' said Vince.

'Ooh, how I LOVES a list! Hand it over, son!' Bob chortled, his roller-skated feet itching with anticipation.

Vince couldn't wait to give the animals what they wanted. Mum had always said it was better to give than to receive, and he was realising what she meant.

Bob scritch-scratched his stubbly chin as he scanned the list with his glinty eyes while Ping stood on a box beside him mouthing all the words . . .

And then they were OFF!

Bob WHIZZED.

Ping FIZZED.

He WHAZZLED.

Ping TWAZZLED.

Bob KERPANGED his way along the length of the counter and back so fast he went blurry.

Ping FITTOOMED up and down the very tall tapering ladder as if her life depended on it.

'TAA-DAAA!' Bob exclaimed, and there before Vince was a huge, higgledy-piggledy heap that looked like EVERYTHING on the list.

'I believe that's EVERYTHING on the list, young whipper-snapper. EXCEPT the denim shorts. We've sold out. We had a rush on them yesterday.'

'Wonderful!' Vince exclaimed as the dust settled. 'How much do I owe you, Bob?' he added, crossing his fingers behind his back that he had enough.

'Ummmmm, let me see . . . That'll be exacterlackerly £9.92. But seeing as it's you – and a very little bird told me it's your birthday –' (Ping blushed poppy red), 'I'll make it £9.91.'

Brilliant! Vince handed over the whole crispy tenner from bad Uncle Stanley (who cared about new trainers anyway?), made sure to get his change and cycled home with his rucksack brimming with booty.

Nine

Gran was in the garden hanging some washing on the line. After pegging up each item she would do a little shimmy – she always danced when she was happy and today Gran was VERY happy.

Vince returned and spotted his

own denim shorts flapping humbly in the breeze amongst all Gran's glamorous frocks.

'Shorts! That's the only thing Bob had sold out of,' said Vince. 'Dave the goat asked for them. They are my favourite shorts, but a goat called Dave's a good cause if ever there was one.'

'Well, that is kind,' said Gran, unpegging the shorts and throwing them to Vince with a wink. 'Very kind indeed, my little pocket prince – Grandpa would be fit to burst!'

As Vince sang his way merrily

through the security gate, Horace
appeared.

'I was hoping it
was you. It is so
nice to have some
intelligent company
for a change,' the old
badger chuntered.

The next piece of this story is
rather hard to divulge.

Actually, I don't even think I can
bear to tell it as it's really horribly

nasty and I would never want to upset you of all people, dear reader.

So, then, it only remains for me to pronounce . . .

THE END

I'd like to thank my fragrant agent and the stern spelling person who helps me (because I'm very bad at spelling) and that nice man who brings the wide selection of sandwiches, savoury snacks and iced buns round my office. Thank you all, and good night.

. . . Hang on.

That's just plain wrong.

We've come this far together, I just KNOW you can handle it.

Besides, it was very lonely without you, dear reader.

So let the story continue. Hold on to your pants!

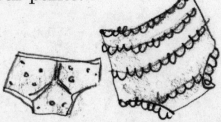

Ten

Now, where were we?

... As Vince and Horace rounded the corner of the penguin pond they heard Asquith shriek, 'He's here and he's carrying a very BIG bag!'

Suddenly, Vince felt like Father

Christmas, and it made him swell out his chest and grow an imaginary beard.

'Batten down the hatches,' rumbled Horace ominously.

Terry the orangutan lumbered up and grabbed (yes – grabbed!) Vince's rucksack off his back.

'That was harsh,' Horace grumbled.

Terry threw out all the gifts as if they were dirty socks from a wash bag.

Vince's denim shorts landed in the pond with a plooosh. Once Terry had found his BULK box of chocolate bananas, he lumbered off reading the small print and muttering,

"Chocolate-flavoured coating" . . . what kind of cheap rubbish is that?'

Hamish the eagle extracted the haggis from the chimney of Asquith's pretend igloo – where it had landed – and merely exclaimed, 'Vegetarian haggis?!

Wha' do ye think I am, laddie, a Sassenach!?'

(I just looked that up in the dictionary. It said 'A Saxon. An Englishman. A Lowlander' – so now we know!)

Dave the goat jiggered forward, grabbed the bunch of clover, sneezed violently in Vince's face and fished the shorts from the pond, exclaiming, 'Not THAT kind of denim, for Pete's sake!' (Who's Pete?) 'It has to be stonewashed!' And then he spat on them. Yes, SPAT on them! TWICE!

'Oh, that's attractive!' said Horace.

Juan the llama was whimpering quietly at this point and staring at the crushed yellow glass of his lemon sweets lying in a dust-puddle of sad sherbet.

'Not eeeven worth licking uuup,' he wept. 'Where's theee drama een that? Theee sweeet sheeeeerbiiity explooosion! GONE! Neeever to reeeeturn!'

(Juan had once worked in the theatre – he was the pantomime llama.)

Janet the owl, who'd eaten a whole mouse in one gulp, had gone into a sugar frenzy and concussed herself by flying into several trees, and was now sitting disconsolately and confused at the edge of the pond, squawking pathetically, 'Well, THESE won't do! String for tails! What are you trying to do? Choke me to death?'

And as for Carol the pig, talk about downright RUDE! She'd simply broken all her eggs into the pond, grunting, 'I meant soft-boiled AND with Marmite soldiers to boot. Stupid boy!'

'Bacon sandwich, anyone?' said Horace.

Vince was speechless.

I told you it was nasty.

Eleven

Vince felt a tear crawl quietly down
one of his cheeks. He had never felt
so tired and disappointed. He'd been
right all along. Animals were
absurd, stinktastic and,
as he now discovered,
downright impolite!

'Oh dear, Vince,' said Horace, spotting his new friend's crumpled face. 'You have to understand they're zoo animals, which means they're all spoilt brats. They have no need to forage, to hunt, to fend for themselves. People pay to visit them and it makes them think they are a cut above wild animals. Their houses are tidied, their bottoms wiped, and they've not had a human who they could ask to get them "STUFF" from outside since your grandpa. It has really brought out the worst in them. I'm awfully sorry. You clearly went to so much trouble AND it's your birthday today, isn't it?'

'Yes, yes it is,' Vince said sadly, thinking of the lack of birthday cake and balloons. Not to mention the lack of Mum and Dad. 'I got this gift from Grandpa, but if I'm honest I've never really been overly keen on animals . . . No offence.'

'None taken,' said Horace, feeling slightly offended.

'I mean, don't get me wrong, I think YOU'RE lovely, Horace, but if you don't mind I just need to go home and think for a bit.'

When Gran saw Vince's face, her earrings immediately lost their sparkle and a whole family of sequins fell off her frock.

And when she heard the story of how horrid and ungrateful all the animals had been, she said some VERY rude words,

which I mustn't write down or I'll get told off. Just think of all the ones you know and times their rudeness by eight and three-quarters.

Vince ran to his room and got Derek the diary. He was feeling so downhearted he couldn't think of anything to say, so he plumphed on to the sofa in the sitting room and decided to write a list of nice things to calm himself down. Like Leviticus Corkindale Percival Calamine Periwig Candlewick Throoob, or

Bob, Vince did love a list.

Favourite things I can see from the sofa today:

1. Mum's collecktion of paperweights (especially the one with the dandelion clock inside).

2. The model snake on the mantelpiece that I made from clay when I was six.

3. The clock with the smiley face.

4. The painting of an orange squirrel eating a nut.

5. The plant with spiky stripy leaves on the sill.

6. My polka-dot sock sticking out from underneath the chair. (So that's where it was!)

7. The candlestick in the shape of a lighthouse.

8. A chocolate orange.

Mmm . . . he might just have to eat some of that.

Shall we leave Vince to recover from his ordeal for the moment, dear reader, and go and see what Horace is getting up to? I think you might be interested. I do hope so.

Twelve

Horace hadn't wasted any time. As soon as he had watched Vince walk through his back door he'd ruffled up his dingy fur to make himself look as large as possible (which wasn't very large, it has to be said) and scrambled up on to the pond wall.

'LISTEN UP YOU 'ORRIBLE LOT!

IT'S YOUR **WILD** FRIEND HERE, AND
LET ME TELL YOU, I'M FEELING **PROPER**
WILD TODAY,

FERAL
FEROCIOUS AND
FIERCE!

I HAVE WITNESSED YOUR BEHAVIOUR IN FLAGRANT TECHNICOLOR GHASTLINESS TODAY.

A FULL-ON DISPLAY OF THE BADDEST MANNERS I HAVE **EVER** HAD THE DISPLEASURE TO BEHOLD.

YOU ARE A COLLECTION OF **GRACELESS**
SCURRILOUS
VULGAR
MOLLYCODDLED

UNGRATEFUL SPOON-FED DEPLORABLE OAFS!!

TODAY IS VINCE'S BIRTHDAY. HIS MUM'S RUN OFF WITH A LION TAMER. I'M **NOT** JOKING. REMEMBER THAT VAIN BLOKE WHO USED TO WORK HERE? WITH THE BOBBLY MUSCLES? ANYWAY...

HIS DAD'S DOWNHEARTED AND SPENDS MORE TIME LOOKING AFTER YOU LOT THAN HIM!

HE SPENT ALL HIS BIRTHDAY MONEY ON STUFF FOR YOU! NOTHING FOR HIM. STUFF FOR YOU!

AND CAN I JUST POINT OUT THAT FAR FROM
EVEN SAYING **"THANK YOU"** OR SHOWING
ANY GRACE OR APPRECIATION WHATSOEVER.
YOU MIGHT AS WELL HAVE KICKED HIM IN THE
YOU-KNOW-WHERES.

YOU HAVE ABUSED
HIS GRANDPA'S GIFT.

YOU MUST MAKE
AMENDS. **OR ELSE** ...

YES ... OR **ELSE** ...

GRrrrrrrrrrrr!

On that last bit Horace really tried to bare his teeth, do a bit of drooling and generally look as threatening as he could, because to be frank he had no idea what course of action he would take if they didn't listen. I mean, let's face it, he was only a badger.

Thirteen

Vince was just tucking into his fifth piece of chocolate orange and starting to feel a little less bleak, when the doorbell rang.

'I'll get it, Gran,' Vince said dolefully.

When Vince opened the door he

was greeted by the sight of a very large, hairy lady in an enormous floral hat.

'Can I help you?' asked Vince kindly, trying not to stare at her moustache.

The lady emitted a curious grunting sound and thrust an envelope into Vince's hand. On it was his name in torn-up bits of newspaper.

'Thank you,' said Vince politely, trying not to grimace at the hairy lady's pungent odour. She lolloped away down the path, adjusting her knickers.

Vince opened the envelope. Inside was an invitation that looked like this:

Fourteen

'Gran! I've been invited to a party at the zoo by a rather hairy lady,' said Vince, walking back into the sitting room.

Gran was looking curiously expectant.

'Oh, what larks! Can I come?' she said.

Gran suggested they ought to dress up if it was a party (not that she needed any excuse). Vince put on his favourite shirt. Can you guess what colour it was?

He topped it off with his Biggles hat covered in badges of all the places they'd caravanned in Cornwall.

Gran put on some earrings that looked like lampshades and her favourite sequinned number in cerise pink. 'I used to inspire whoops from the punters in this, Vince,' she told him proudly, adding, 'In case I step in anything unsavoury,' as she pointed to her wellington-booted feet.

The two of them looked a picture heading down the garden path in the twilight, Gran's sequinned tassley frock twinkling like a sparkler.

It felt unusually quiet as Vince and Gran went through the gate, with no Horace to greet them even. A mysteriously 'held' atmosphere.

'It feels unusually quiet, Gran,' said Vince.

'It certainly does, my priceless plum duff. Are we unfashionably early?'

Just then, Horace appeared, a tad out of breath and sporting a small bow tie.

'I believe you had an invitation.

Do walk this way,'
he said formally.

If you were
to see the sight
that greeted

Vince and Gran as they walked
towards Asquith's pond, I think
you'd let out as sizeable a gasp as
they did. Across the pond was a
string of bunting that looked like
it had been made entirely out of
different coloured pants (if you've
ever had any pants disappear from

your washing line, you now know where they might have gone). It was lit up with a magical light coming from clutches of hovering fireflies.

In the warm glow stood a line of very contrite animals, their various fuzzy, furry, feathery heads hanging low, bowed in shame.

As they saw Vince and Gran approaching they all started to ruffle and shuffle and clear their throats. Asquith (who was cutting a fine

dash in a silk waistcoat and some velvet slippers with an embroidered 'A' on them) rapped an old ice-cream stick three times on the wall, looking extremely serious. And then, dear reader, they all did something rather unexpected . . .

They all began to sing!

THE SORRY SONG

Oh Vince, dear Vince,

what joy you bring!

You got your gift –

a precious thing.

You came to us,

we were soooo rude,

but now check out our attitude!

We thank you,

thank you from our hearts.

We've been like brats,

spoilt brutes,

upstarts,

But coz of YOU

we've changed our ways,

[change of key] learnt gratitude,

oh happy days!

We're sorry, Vince,

[Terry's solo line] you awesome dude.

You made us see

we were so crude.

You learnt us that

we'd gone all wrong.

You made us want

to sing a song!

We'd lost the plot,

we'd dropped the ball,

we wasn't being kind at all.

We'd pipped the squeak,

we'd blocked the pipe,

become the spoilt and ghastly type.

We'd locked the door

and lost a key,

we'd spilt the milk

and cried 'Yippeeeee'

coz someone else would clear the mess –

we got to caring less and less.

Oh thank you, Vince!

We'll make you love

the gift you have.

Our wish is this!

We weren't worth

talking to before but

now we hope that

you might miss

us if you ever

went away

but say you won't

not soon at least

oh happy day!

Vince, please accept

this song our sorry and . . .

OUR FEAST!

'What was that about?' hissed Gran. 'It had a very catchy beat.'

'They were saying sorry, Gran. It was a sorry song,' Vince replied, feeling rather special.

'I should think so, too,' she murmured with feeling.

'I should think so, three!' said Horace.

With that, Asquith took a very deep bow, and the choir stood back to reveal a rickety trestle table covered in some dubious-looking party snacks.

Fifteen

The party feast array kicked off with three dead mice courtesy of Janet the owl.

'They're not the best lookers, dearest, but I can assure you they are utterly divine!

I've been saving them for a special occasion.'

'Ooh, how generous, Janet, thank you,' said Vince, wondering how long she had kept them and feeling quietly revolted.

There was some cud from Juan. 'Eeeet's pre-digested food, Veeence, an acquired taste but I am confident yooou weeel beee mad for eeeeet!'

'I'm sure it will be an absolute delicacy, Juan, how kind!' Vince said, rather too brightly.

Some 'slop' in a
bowl from Carol
the pig. 'That's
a particularly
fine vintage, Vince.
I sometimes save a bowl to ferment
a bit. I find it really brings out the
tangy flavours.'

'I don't know about you, but I
think it's the word "tangy" in that
sentence that most disturbs me,'
said Horace.

'I LOVE tangy!' piped Vince.

Two shiny
mackerel from
Asquith – 'Slips
down a treat, old pal, you barely
have to chew!'

A dried banana. 'I've been saving
this one in my belly button for
someone special,' said Terry, proudly.

'I think I might throw up,' Horace
chuntered.

'Shhhh!' hushed Vince.

A piece of goat horn from Dave.
'It fell off the other day, Vince.

I thought it might make a nice pendant. I did TRY to eat it but I've got to be honest, it tastes revolting.'

'You surprise me,' Horace chuckled.

'Just what I've always wanted!' said Vince, almost meaning it.

Some real haggis from Hamish. 'I dinnae know how a managed tae stop masel' polishing it off, Vince! It's made out o' the innards o' a sheep! Suuuperb!'

Vince felt quite pale but grinned widely and said, 'YUM.'

'That was convincing,' said Horace sarcastically.

Some jelly from Fenella. (It was the raspberry packet Vince had given her, with a beaky bite taken out of it.) Vince was now feeling extremely moved, although curiously he suddenly didn't feel peckish at all. He wished Dad could be there to share this most momentous of birthdays. He simply couldn't wait to tell him all the extraordinary news.

Gran had been having one of her little 'Happy Cries' about Grandpa. She didn't understand the animals but she remembered what it had been like being with Grandpa Jacko when he spoke to them, and her chest was so puffed with joy as she watched Vince that it made one of her necklaces ping off and scatter.

One bead actually concussed

an unsuspecting
sparrow.

'Happy birthday, Vince!' the
animals chorused.

'What are they saying?' hissed
Gran.

'They're saying happy birthday,
Gran.'

With that, Terry the orangutan
stepped forward. 'Let's get this
party started!' he exclaimed, hitting
a button on an ancient CD player.
A wild Irish jig crackled out into

the twilight and Terry got down on one knee, proffering a hairy hand to Gran. 'Would you give me the honour of this dance, oh ancient spangly lady?'

'What's he saying?' croaked Gran.

'He wants to dance with you, Gran.'

'Is he aware I'm a professional?' shrieked Gran as Terry swung her round and began to boogaloo.

Asquith and Vince danced pogo-style.

Janet the owl and Hamish the eagle did the mashed potato.

Juan the llama and Dave the goat started to boogie-woogie.

Carol the pig and Fenella the flamingo hokey-cokeyed their way around the pond.

Suddenly, the big fat rays of a torch sparkled from the distance in the twilight.

'Quick, hide!' they all hissed. 'Someone's coming!' The fireflies turned off as if someone had flicked

a switch and the animals couldn't be seen for dust.

'What did they say?' exclaimed Gran, just as Terry the orangutan appeared and scooped her up in his arms. 'I'll look after the crinkly lady, Vince!' he whispered.

'Oooh, I've always liked a bit of hair on a man,' Gran confided as Terry lifted her away into the shadows.

Vince swung around desperately, trying to see where he could hide, while the torch light danced closer.

'Over here,' Horace hissed. 'Ever been down a badger sett before?'

Sixteen

Closer and closer the dancing light came.

Vince, Gran and the animals held their breaths in their respective hiding places.

Horace did quite a loud burp.

'Pardon me,' he whispered to

Vince's feet. 'I had sweetcorn for breakfast.'

'Shhhhhh,' hissed Vince sternly.

'MUM? VINCE?' the torch shouted.

IT WAS DAD!

Vince oozed out of Horace's hall, feeling like a toothpaste boy coming out of a tube. 'Dad! It's us! Over here!'

But Dad looked VERY cross.

'What are you playing at? I've been worried sick! Is Gran with you?!'

'Yes, poppet, here I am!' exclaimed Gran, adjusting her hat as Terry gently lowered her to the ground, much to Dad's complete astonishment.

'What have you two been up to?!'

Gran piped up, 'We've been to a birthday party.'

'Whose?' said Dad irritably, genuinely forgetting in that moment that it was Vince's birthday today.

'MINE,' said Vince.

There was a VERY long pause. In fact, it was THIS long:

Actually it was even longer but I didn't want to waste too much paper and be responsible for the end of the rainforest as we know it.

'I'm so, so sorry, Vince,' Dad said, rubbing his furrowed brow. 'This hasn't been a great birthday for you, and it's all my fault.'

'Dad, it's been my BEST BIRTHDAY EVER!' said Vince wholeheartedly. 'I got Grandpa's gift!'

Dad looked visibly startled.

'I think you might have startled your dad, Vince,' said Horace knowingly.

'The talking to the animals one! I'm fluent in Animal, Dad!'

Seventeen

'I'm so happy for you, son!' Dad exclaimed, looking properly happy for the first time in months. 'Your grandpa said it would happen but I didn't believe him.'

If there's a moral to this story – which there isn't – but IF there was, it would be that often we don't really listen to crinkly old people but maybe we should.

(Unless they're horrid, in which case I wouldn't bother listening whatever age they are.)

Then Vince and Gran told Dad the whole story of their extraordinary day, which I shan't write down because you've just read it all and that would

be repeating myself.

And then the animals did a reprise of their song. Which to Dad and Gran, of course, just sounded like animals making the sort of noises they make in the night, only a tad more organised and with quite an impressive percussion section.

And then Vince, Dad and Gran waved goodnight and blew kisses and had a few hugs and it all got a bit emotional like happy endings can.

And Dad gave Vince a piggyback home. (Why ARE they called that? Must ask Carol the pig.)

And they sang the Zoo Keepers' Song as a duet to get through the gate . . .

OH! Just remembered!

YES, dear reader! Permission HAS been granted by the relevant authorities at last! I can share the Zoo Keepers' Song, but only with YOU, because YOU know the story. Do NOT divulge this song to ANYONE on pain of being put in a trunk with an elephant with no trunk who will poo perilously close to you and try and chew your cheeks . . .

THE ZOO KEEPERS' SONG

We are the zoo keepers, yippety yip.

We're mad about all animals and

full of vim and vip.

We love the feathers, wool and fur

(if you stroke us we will purr).

We love the hooves, the wings,

the claws, that animals,

they don't do wars.

We love the beaks and fins
and tails,
It's a job that never fails
to thriiiiill!
(We call a vet if they are ill!)

We are the zoo keepers,
flappety flooop.
We have a hut and microwave for
warming up our soup.

Those 'Private' signs don't mean
a thing

(doors open to us when we sing).

The 'Don't do . . .' signs,
they're not for us
(coz we're allowed, no sweat,
no fuss).

'Hands off the bars' –
words we ignore.
We'll even touch a lion's paw,
it's truuuue!
(We do not recommend
YOU do!)

We are the zoo keepers,
zippety zam.
We live so near the premises
that we don't need a van.

If they poo we clean it up
(coz we're not squeamish,
we are tough).
If they bite it's never sore.
(Ever seen a zoo keeper cry
before?)

The beasts are wind
beneath our sails,
It's a job that never
fails to glowww!
(Although we wish it
paid more dough!)

Remember your promise!

Zoo keepers the world over are
watching you.

Epilogue

When Dad and Gran and Vince got
home, Dad remembered that he'd
forgotten that he'd remembered to
get a VERY LARGE birthday cake
for Vince, absolutely covered in
wonderful orange icing with Vince's
name on AND the number 8 written

out in coloured sprinkles. They ate
way too much of it, and they stayed
up way too late, because sometimes
things like Christmas and birthdays
and finding out you have powers
beyond your wildest imaginings
mean you HAVE to do that . . .

And Dad really laughed and laughed for the first time in AGES.

AND Vince told Dad every minute detail of the day until his jaws ached, and they sang the Zoo Keepers' Song together as a duet over and over.

AND Gran opened the sherry and did so many toasts she got the hiccups and had to drink a whole beaker of squash backwards.

AND last but by no means least, Vince finally thanked Dad very, very much for his precious birthday

goldfish and named him Jacko . . .
after Grandpa.

And that really is . . .

The Acknowledgements Song

Oh them peeps at Faber
They are a JOY
Leah Thaxton (she's not a boy)
She let me in
She gave me tea
She decided she could work with me . . .

Oh YAY, Oh Yay
Oh lucky me
Fiddlee Doo Da
Fiddley Dee

Oh Alice Swan (she's not a bird)
She let me stay
She listened and heard
She's frightfully clever
I hope it rubs off
She gives you top tips
And lets you show off

Oh Emma and Will
They gone and dun ART
They really both are
Frightfully smart
They sort it all out
All them letters and pics
(Occasionally they stop for bics)

Thanking thee Faber
Thanking thee all
You are a top team
Some quite small, some quite tall
Thank you for welcoming me
Into your den
Full of such clever wimmin and men

Agents up Curtis Bee . . .
Lauren P and Stephanie T
Oh fragrant dolls both
You make it make sense
Past, present and future
You take away tense
Thank you for taking
This dodgy turn on
Thank you for inspiring a verse of this song

Richard James Lumsden
For the maps all unfurled
For guiding and teaching
A whole new world . . .

Rebecca Ashdown, eek
What can I say
You've literally made
A dream come true
In your inimitable way

And now for my Dad
Who is worlds apart
But never, never out of my heart
Thank you, my Magic Roundabout man
As a stinky badger you have been cast
The pedestal could never last!

Fa la la la
and pooty ma loot
This Acknowledgements Song
Has sung its last toot!

DON'T MISS THE NEXT

ZOO BOY

ADVENTURE!

COMING SOON . . .